THE Great Train MYSTERY

First Edition

Published by Gallopade International/Carole Marsh Books. Printed in the United States of America.

Editor: Janice Baker
Assistant Editor: Gabrielle Humphrey
Cover Design: Vicki DeJoy
Content Design: Randolyn Friedlander

Gallopade International is introducing SAT words that kids need to know in each new book that we publish. The SAT words are bold in the story. Look for each word in the special SAT glossary. Happy Learning!!

Gallopade is proud to be a member and supporter of these educational organizations and associations:

American Booksellers Association
American Library Association
International Reading Association
National Association for Gifted Children
The National School Supply and Equipment Association
The National Council for the Social Studies
Museum Store Association
Association of Partners for Public Lands
Association of Booksellers for Children
Association for the Study of African American Life and History
National Alliance of Black School Educators

Once upon a time...

Write one about spiders!

Papa said ...
Why don't you set the stories in real locations?
Mystery
That's a great idea! And if I do that, I might as well choose real kids as characters in the stories! But which kids would I pick?
MiMi, PiCK ME, PiCK ME!
ME, TOO, MiMi, PiCK ME, TOO!
Christina
Grant
Pick me!

You two really are characters, that's all I've got to say!

Yes you are! And, of course I choose you! But what should I write about?

National Parks!

Famous Places!

FUN PLACES!

Disney World!

New York City!

Dracula's Castle

On the *Mystery Girl* airplane ...

I can FLY us anywhere!

Or aboard the *Mimi*!

Or by surfboard, rickshaw, motorbike, camel ...

All great ideas! I can put a lot of history, MYSTERY, legend, lore, and **laughs** in the books! We can use other boys and girls in the books. It will be educational and fun!

Good stuff!

And can you put some cool stuff online? Like a Book Club and a Scavenger Hunt and a Map so we can track our adventures?

And so, Mimi, Papa, Christina, and Grant took off aboard the *Mystery Girl* and America's National Mystery Book Series—where the adventure is real and so are the characters! —was born.

START YOUR ADVENTURE TODAY!

1
PROMO WHAT SUMMIT?

"Hey, what's up, sis?" Grant asked his older sister Christina. He plopped down next to her on the hotel bed.

The sudden movement of the bouncy mattress sent Christina's laptop dancing. She caught it just before it hit the floor.

"Grant, *please* don't do that!" she pleaded.

"Whoa, that was close!" Grant exclaimed.

The air conditioner sensed the rising temperature in the room and came to life. It blew cool air into their hotel suite. The floor-length curtains billowed in and out in a slow, rhythmic dance, occasionally revealing the busy Washington, D.C., street corner outside their hotel.

"What are you reading anyway?" he asked.

Christina was getting annoyed. She looked hard at her little brother. His curly blond hair was already getting long. Summer was halfway through, and they hadn't set foot in their local hair salon in over a month.

"You're being nosy again, Grant," she said matter-of-factly. Christina turned her attention back to the screen. She wore her long, brown hair pulled back loosely in her favorite clip. She blew a stray hair off her face.

Grant really didn't like being called "nosy" by his sister, but he couldn't help it. He just *had* to know.

"Graaant, I know you're trying to read over my shoulder. If you don't stop it, I'm telling Mimi," Christina warned.

Grant stood up. "If you'd just *tell* me, you wouldn't have to tell *on* me," he suggested, laughing at his play on words.

"Gosh, you're persistent!" Christina exclaimed.

Mimi was on her cell phone, pacing the floor between their adjoining hotel rooms.

"Yes, I understand. Union Station. 8 p.m." Mimi snapped her cell phone shut and smiled. "Children, I just got off the phone with Papa's good friend, John Goodfellow. His steam train, *The General*, is being readied for our cross-country departure this very evening!"

Mimi and Papa, Grant and Christina's grandparents, often invited them on special trips like this one. Papa would fly them all over the place in his red-and-white airplane, the *Mystery Girl*, so Mimi, a children's mystery writer, could do research for her books. But this vacation would be very different!

"Wait, Mimi!" Christina interrupted. "So this isn't just any old museum train? This is a real-live working train? And we're crossing the country in it?"

"To just outside Promontory Summit, Utah!" Mimi answered.

"Promo *what* Summit?" Grant asked.

"Promontory Summit," Mimi repeated. "Mr. Goodfellow heard I was writing a children's mystery on the history of the railway and Westward Expansion in the United States," Mimi explained. "He just offered to let us take his train across the country. And what better way to gather research, right? I think it's a fabulous idea, and so does Papa!"

"We get to experience what it must have been like over one hundred years ago, traveling west across the country in a real steam train!" Christina exclaimed.

"If only we could meet real cowboys and Indians from the Wild West!" Grant shouted. "And even go on a real cattle drive!"

Mimi smiled. "Riding the cattle trails was hard work–and dangerous. Even so, the journals left behind by real cowhands all seemed to say the same thing–that they couldn't imagine doing anything else!"

Christina was thoughtful. "When trains began transporting cattle long distances, was that the end of the long cattle drives?"

"That," Mimi agreed, "and the fact that ranchers on the Great Plains began fencing in their property with barbed wire to control where their cattle grazed. The open range was becoming, well, not-so-open, and access to the cattle trails was cut off."

"Still," Grant insisted, "cowboys worked on ranches, right? And performed in rodeos!"

"True! All was not lost!" Mimi agreed.

"Yee haw!" Grant slapped his knee to a tune only he could hear.

Mimi chuckled.

"What's Promontory Summit, anyway?" Grant asked.

"Good question, Grant," Papa bellowed.

Their grandfather ducked slightly to fit his tall frame through the doorway. He stretched his arms way above his head and yawned.

"Promontory Summit is where the eastern and western railways met to form the First Transcontinental Railroad nearly 150 years ago!" Papa explained. "The two lines linked both ends of the United States! It was a very big deal!"

Mimi scooted over towards Papa and took his hand. "Gone were the days of crossing the country by covered wagon, which could take six months easily," she said.

"And that's if you made it across alive!" Papa added.

Mimi said, "A collector of old steam locomotives has been after Mr. Goodfellow for years to sell him *The General*. Mr. Goodfellow feels it's time to let her go."

2

UNION STATION, HERE WE COME!

KNOCK KNOCK KNOCK! "Room service!"

"We ordered dinner in–burgers and fries from the hotel restaurant," Mimi said.

"Yum! I'll get it!" Grant offered. He sprinted towards the door. "Coooooming!" he yelled.

Papa caught Grant. "Remember, be polite. Here's the tip." Papa slipped a five-dollar bill into Grant's hand.

Midway through their meal, Grant asked, "Papa, steam engines aren't used anymore, are they?"

"Not really," Papa answered. "They're not practical for long distances. Diesel-powered engines use less manpower, can haul more, and can go faster."

"So, driving Mr. Goodfellow's steam train is a really big honor?" Grant asked.

"Absolutely!" Papa answered. "But engineers actually 'pilot' a train; they don't 'drive' it."

"I see! Hey, I've got a joke for you," said Grant. "What's the difference between a teacher and a steam train?"

"Don't know. What?" Papa asked.

"The teacher tells you to spit out your gum, but the train says, 'choo choo choo'!" Grant replied, giggling.

Papa chuckled and checked his watch. "Be ready in fifteen," he said. "I'll call the porter now."

Christina stacked the dinner plates and glasses onto the hotel tray and placed the tray outside their door for room service to collect.

A shiny piece of paper lying on the floor caught her eye. It was glittered with gold flecks and oddly shaped, like a perfect, oversized puzzle piece.

Christina heard some rustling at the end of the hall. She turned to see a man wearing a blue uniform and a black train engineer's cap turn suddenly and run straight into the wall. He looked her way, pulled his cap low over his eyes, and crawled out of sight.

That was weird! she thought. Christina slipped the paper into her backpack and finished packing her things.

KNOCK KNOCK KNOCK!

"Union Station, here we come! Chugga chugga choo choo!" Grant cheered wildly. Christina couldn't help but smile at her little brother's antics.

Papa entered Grant and Christina's room wearing his signature Stetson cowboy hat, leather boots, and blue jeans. Shadowing Papa was an aging porter with "Gary" printed in fading letters across his nametag. Gary hobbled into the room, pushing an oversized bellman's cart. He expertly loaded their suitcases onto the cart, but left a small section uncovered.

The *click click click* of Mimi's favorite red cowboy boots on the tile floor announced her arrival.

"All right!" Papa roared. "Is everyone ready for a good old-fashioned train adventure aboard *The General*?"

"Yes, sir!" the kids shouted. They bounded towards the door.

Christina noticed the porter's eyes widen and then narrow. Beads of sweat formed on his forehead. He quickly changed his expression, though, to one of feigned disinterest and turned his attention to Grant.

"Want a lift?" Gary offered, pointing to the uncovered spot on the bellman's cart.

"Thanks!" Grant replied and hopped onto the cart. Everyone piled into the elevator on their way to a blue-and-white cab waiting at the hotel entrance.

As the cab pulled out into the heavy evening traffic, Porter Gary shuffled back inside the lobby of the brightly lit hotel, his cell phone pinned close to his ear.

3

A WELCOME CHANGE!

On the taxi ride over to the D.C. Union Station, Grant convinced Mimi to sit in the middle so he could fog up the window and draw weird faces with his finger.

"Union Station!" the cab driver announced after awhile.

They tumbled out into a sea of commuters on their way home. The sweltering heat made it difficult to breathe.

The grand Union Station towered above them. It was lit up like a beacon in the night. A row of American flags waved down at them.

"He's not picking up!" Mimi sounded worried. "Tony, Mr. Goodfellow's assistant, is supposed to meet us." She punched redial.

"Papa, the station is beautiful!" Christina exclaimed. She perched next to her brother on the luggage.

Papa agreed. "It was modeled after stations built in Europe at the time. See the arches and the sculptures? Union Station is more than one hundred years old."

Mimi walked over and handed her cell phone to Papa.

"No luck?" Papa asked. "Let me give it a try."

"What are those sculptures up there?" Christina asked Mimi, pointing to just above the entrance arches.

Mimi answered, "Those sculptures represent all of the things that America was built on: fire, electricity, freedom, imagination, agriculture, and mechanics."

"Yep," Papa said. He handed Mimi her cell phone and gave her a thumbs up. "Union Station was a welcome change for the residents of this area. Instead of having to go to one of several different stations scattered around the city, the D.C. Union Station combined all the stations into one. Even the track running through the Mall was removed," Papa added.

"You mean trains used to run through a shopping mall?" Grant asked. "No way!"

"I think Papa's talking about the National Mall, where the Washington Monument and the Lincoln Memorial are," Christina said.

"Trains really went through there?" Grant asked.

"It's hard to imagine, but true," Mimi said. "The residents of our nation's capital were proud of this station. People from all over the world came to see it–and still do."

Christina scooted closer to her brother. "Want to know what I was reading about at the hotel?"

Grant nodded.

"Well, a long time ago, a very wealthy man from Bethel, Vermont, opened a granite quarry," she explained. "He was at the **zenith** of his career. He had a wife and son who he loved more than life itself.

"But, one day," she continued, "his son was killed in a horrible railroad crossing accident! The man was heartbroken!

"From that day forward, he vowed that all granite from his quarry would be used for nothing but *tombstones*!" Christina whispered the word 'tombstones.'

"Tombstones?" Grant echoed.

"Uh huh. But, there's more," she said. "After the man died, Bethel Granite changed hands. And whether the new owners knew of the vow or not, much of the granite used to build the outer walls of Union Station is believed to have come from *that very quarry*." Grant's face went sheet white.

"Grant, don't worry! It's probably just a legend–" Christina said, hoping she hadn't scared her little brother.

Grant was watching a tall, elderly gentleman wearing an old-fashioned wool cap and tweed suit.

Christina rubbed her eyes. *No way! Is that his ghost?* she wondered.

"It's the Bethel ghost dad!" cried Grant.

“Grant, shhh!” Christina whispered. “He’s coming over here!”

“Mr. Goodfellow!” Mimi cried.

Both Grant and Christina let out an audible sigh of relief.

“John!” Papa said, “It’s so good to see you! You’ve had a change of heart?”

“Not a chance!” Mr. Goodfellow said with a twang in his voice and a twinkle in his gray-blue eyes.

“Tony, my assistant, called. Something about traffic. Anyway, I’m here to escort you to *The General*!” the old man explained.

“Well, thank you, John! What an adventure this will be!” Mimi said.

Despite Mr. Goodfellow’s winter attire in the dead of summer, he showed no signs of being uncomfortable.

“John, these are our grandchildren, Grant and Christina,” Mimi said.

Mr. Goodfellow tipped his hat at Grant and shook his hand. Then, just as he had done to Mimi, he took Christina’s hand, leaned down, and gave it a kiss. Christina blushed.

"Be sure to get into plenty of mischief, you hear?" Mr. Goodfellow said with a smile.

Grant and Christina shared a look of surprise and then burst out laughing. Mr. Goodfellow winked at the kids. He picked up two of the heaviest suitcases.

"Now, John, you don't have to carry those things," Papa said, as he quickly demonstrated the pull-out handle-and-wheels feature on the suitcases.

Mr. Goodfellow laughed heartily. "What'll they come up with next?" he exclaimed.

4
THE DISAPPEARING ACT

Union Station was even more impressive on the inside. It was late, but sightseers continued to pour in from all entrances. They snapped photos of the intricate, domed ceiling and original stained-glass windows.

"For an old man, Mr. Goodfellow is fast!" Grant said, as they hurried to keep up with Papa's friend.

"Are you sure it's John's age that's keeping him from going with us on this trip?" Mimi whispered to Papa.

"He does keep us guessing, doesn't he?" Papa replied.

They wound their way through more corridors. The *tap shuffle tap shuffle* of Mr. Goodfellow's boot heels against the shiny floor resonated throughout the halls.

"This way, folks!" he called. Then he disappeared. They made a run for it and rounded the corner.

"Huh?" Grant exclaimed. "He's gone!"

"It's a dead end!" Christina cried.

"John came this way, I'm sure of it," Mimi said.

"Well, if you can't go over or under these walls, you have to go through them, right?" Grant deduced.

He gently pushed on the wall panels. "Over here, everyone!" he yelled. One of the panels swung open like some secret door into a huge, dimly lit glass dome.

"Wow! Good work, Grant!" everyone cheered. Papa patted him on the back.

"Look up!" Christina cried.

Running the length of the dome, high above them, was a gleaming track. And resting on the track in the shadows was a magnificent black steam locomotive.

Just then, the mammoth engine came to life! Christina ducked and threw up her arms, afraid the glass dome would shatter into a million pieces and come raining down on them.

"This way, children!" Papa shouted. They climbed the spiral staircase to train level.

Christina looked over the rail. "Look," Christina gasped. She grabbed her brother's shirttail before he could get away. "Our suitcases! Come on!"

The kids scrambled back down the stairs two-by-two. There, behind the stairwell, were two suitcases. Mimi's appeared untouched. Papa's, on the other hand, looked like an oyster split wide open, its contents spilled out onto the dusty floor.

The kids quickly shoved Papa's belongings back into the bag. Christina fiddled with the zipper, but it was stuck. "Oh, it's just Papa's ID tag," Christina murmured to herself.

"Let's get a move on," Papa called down from the top of the stairwell. "Oh, you found our bags!"

The children waved to their grandfather. "That's weird," Grant said. "Why would Mr. Goodfellow leave their bags here? And why was Papa's suitcase open?"

"I don't know, but Mr. Goodfellow wasn't alone," Christina said.

"How do you know?" Grant asked.

Christina pointed to a second set of shoeprints in the dust. "Mr. Goodfellow was wearing snake-skinned cowboy boots. These prints were made from some other kind of boot." An impression of a series of circles could be seen plainly in the dust.

Grant stared at his sister with his mouth agape. "You should be a detective!"

"Thanks! Take a look at this!" Christina said. She showed Grant the attached ID tag.

"What is it?" Grant asked.

Christina pulled out the golden piece of paper, unfolded it, and exclaimed, "Just as I thought!"

"Huh?" Grant asked.

"I'll explain later." She refolded the puzzle-shaped paper and slipped it into her backpack. "For now, let's get these bags up the stairs!" she urged.

If Christina had looked up, she would have seen a man peering down at them from the train above. He was frowning. He wore his cap pulled down low over his eyes.

5
ALL ABOARD!

The General was magnificent close up. The giant, black wheels dwarfed the children, making Grant and Christina feel *very* small. The attached train cars snaked along the glistening track and disappeared inside a dark tunnel.

"Whoa!" Grant exclaimed. "This is awesome!"

To Christina, Grant looked the way he did on Christmas morning. It made her smile.

"There's a whistle–a real whistle just like the one on my model trains at home! And there's a headlamp and a smokestack!" Grant shouted.

"Isn't she a beauty?" Papa yelled over the train's din and rattle. "It was built in 1892 and modeled after the movie star locomotive, *The Sierra No. 3.*"

Just then, Mimi said, "Luke, the train engineer, says that Mr. Goodfellow was called away on business, so we'll meet up with him in Utah as planned."

A man with gray-flecked hair appeared in the cab window. He wore blue-and-white striped overalls, a red kerchief around his neck, and a black engineer's cap.

"Ah, there's Engineer Luke now!" Papa announced.

He gave Papa the thumbs up.

Papa hollered, "All aboard!"

The train lurched forward. It screeched and bellowed.

TOOT! TOOT! The whistle blew.

CLICKETY-CLACK! CLICKETY-CLACK! The track rose and fell under the weight of the massive train.

"Hang on!" Mimi said. "We're off!"

Christina felt like she was in a giant snow globe. But, instead of snow, the smoke and steam billowing from the smokestack filled the dome with thick, white clouds.

Just then, a man wearing a hotel uniform shuffled along the train platform, shaking an angry fist in the air.

Porter Gary? Why would he follow us here? Christina wondered.

"Oh, my goodness!" Mimi cried. "Where's Grant?"

Christina hurried to the front of the observation car. "Look, he's still on the platform!" she squealed.

Grant wore the frightened look of a small child lost at an amusement park. He was running as quickly as he could alongside the train.

Papa opened the door. "Grant, grab the rail!" he yelled.

Grant reached up, legs pumping fast. He grabbed onto the rail, just as the giant glass dome yawned open. A rush of warm, summer air blew in.

Papa grabbed onto Grant's arm and yanked him inside. Christina slid the door shut and exhaled loudly.

"Grant, now what were you thinking?" Papa scolded.

Mimi added, “You could have been left behind, or worse, hurt!”

Panting, Grant dropped to his knees and flipped onto his back, trying hard to catch his breath.

“Papa...Mimi...I’m...sorry,” Grant said and sat up.

“Well, at least you’re safe. That’s all that matters,” Mimi said tenderly.

Grant joined his sister at the window. “That was pretty scary!” he exclaimed.

“You OK?” Christina asked.

“I am now!” Grant answered.

“Good!” she said, and punched him in the arm.

“Ouch! What was that for?” Grant asked.

“For scaring Mimi half to death!” she replied.

“OK, I deserved that!” he admitted. They both laughed.

Grant said, “Hey, do you want to watch the dome close?”

Christina nodded. “Mimi, may we?” she asked.

"Absolutely! Go on!" she urged.

"But," Papa warned, "be careful crossing between the train cars. We don't want to lose anyone!"

"OK, Papa! We'll be careful!" the kids promised.

"I'll go check in with Luke," Papa announced. He removed his cowboy hat and replaced it with a black train engineer's cap.

"You are a man of many hats!" Mimi said, smiling at her husband.

Papa tipped his hat to her. "That I am!"

The kids raced to the end of the observation car, laughing. Grant slid the door open.

"Whoa! I can see the track!" Grant cried, bracing himself against the door to keep from falling between the cars.

"Just hang onto the rail when you cross," Christina instructed.

They tiptoed through the dining car, where a heavy-set woman wearing a blue uniform and a white apron was busy folding cloth napkins at a table.

She had bright blue eyes and freshly scrubbed cheeks. "Come on by a little later on," she said. "I'll be serving a little dessert before bedtime."

"Yes, ma'am!" said Grant and Christina. "We will!"

Next, they glided through an elegant Victorian-style club car. Christina admired the red velvet love seat and lace curtains. "Mimi will probably pick this place to write!" Christina guessed.

They bounded through the sleeper car. "Look! Bunk beds!" Grant shouted.

They moved to the next car. "This must be the baggage car!" Christina exclaimed. It had a musty smell. Worn, leather suitcases were piled high along one length of the car. A large, wooden crate stood in a corner.

Grant tried the door to the next car. "It's locked!" He sounded disappointed.

"Let me try," Christina said. The door wouldn't budge. She reached up and felt along the top of the door frame. "Aha! A key!" she exclaimed. CLICK!

"Wow, it worked!" Grant said.

"I know! I never cease to amaze myself!" Christina joked and returned the key to its hiding place. She slid the door open and screamed!

Facing them was a fierce, full-size stuffed bear. Several other animals were mounted like trophies on the walls.

Grant laughed. "They're not alive, Christina!"

"I know that! Yogi Bear just took me by surprise, that's all!" Christina cried. Her heart was pounding through her shirt.

"That's not Yogi Bear!" Grant said, shaking his head.

A towering glass bookcase, stuffed with thick, important-looking books, stood behind a mahogany desk. "This must be Mr. Goodfellow's private car," Christina guessed.

They traveled to the end of the bright-red caboose. Christina's hair came loose from her clip and blew around wildly as the train picked up speed.

"Woo hoo!" they yelled, pumping their fists high in the air.

"Look, Grant! The dome! It's closing!" Christina shouted.

The glass dome of the station closed, leaving the night sky in its wake. To the outside world, Christina guessed the dome looked like an oversized planetarium. She wondered what adventures awaited them on this train journey to the West!

6

UNWELCOME RESIDENT?

"Race you back?" Grant challenged his sister.

"You're on!" Christina said.

Getting back through the train was a lot faster this time.

"Our suitcases!" Grant said, as they bounded through their sleeper car. He pointed to some unfamiliar bags. Christina shrugged.

Grant opened the door to the observation car. "We're back! We saw the dome close! It was—" Grant stopped. Standing beside Mimi were two children Grant and Christina's ages, and the woman from the dining car.

"Oh, good. You're back!" Mimi said with a smile. "This is Miss Tess, and this is Paul and Anna."

The boy wore a baseball cap and carried a baseball in his right hand. The girl had short blonde hair, like her brother. Anna wore shorts and a cute flower-patterned top. She smiled at Christina.

Paul announced, “We’ve never traveled with kids our own ages before! We can show you all of the good hiding places.”

“OK!” Grant exclaimed.

“Anyone up for dessert, follow me!” Miss Tess commanded. Everyone followed and the kids sat together at one of the tables in the dining car.

“This apple pie is delicious!” Christina exclaimed. “Your mom is an excellent cook!”

“Miss Tess isn’t our mom,” Anna said.

“Huh?” Christina replied.

“I see you like apple pie!” Miss Tess noted.

“Your pie is delicious–the best I’ve ever had!” Christina admitted.

“So happy you enjoyed it!” Then, she lowered her voice and leaned in. “The secret’s in the apple–the softer, the better!” She turned to refill Mimi’s water glass.

After chatting and giggling with their new friends for a while longer, Grant and Christina were ready for bed. "Good night, Mimi and Papa!" Christina said.

Papa said, "Don't be alarmed if you feel the train stop in the middle of the night from time to time. At about two in the morning, Engineer Luke will stop for water in Cincinnati, Ohio."

"A water stop?" Grant asked. He spied Papa's glass filled to the brim with ice water. "But won't Miss Tess give him water?"

Papa chuckled. "The train–not Engineer Luke–needs a water stop."

Grant's face reddened. "I knew that!"

"Of course you did, Grant!" Papa exclaimed. "And what do steam engines need water for?" he asked.

Grant's eyes lit up. "To make steam!" he answered.

"That's right!" Papa said. "Steam engines use coal, wood, or oil to heat the water to make steam. The pressurized steam is what drives the train and even sounds the whistles."

"Wow!" Christina exclaimed. "What kind of fuel does *The General* use, Papa?"

"The train used to carry coal to heat the water, but it was converted to carry oil. It's much cleaner and more efficient than having to shovel coal into a firebox all day!" Papa explained.

Papa handed Grant two walkie talkies. "These might come in handy, especially if you are on either ends of the train."

"Cool! Thanks, Papa," Grant said and handed Christina hers. They ran to catch up to their friends.

Once inside the sleeper car, Grant dove onto the bottom bunk. "We can't wait to see those hiding places you were talking about, Paul!" he said.

"Sure! We'll just have to remember to stay out of Danfy's way, though," Paul warned.

"Danfy?" Grant mumbled and yawned.

"It's just what we call him," Paul answered.

"We're guessing he's about as old as the train," Anna said, "which is about 120 years old."

Grant and Christina shared a puzzled look.

"People don't usually get that old," Grant stated.

"No, they don't," Paul agreed, "but ghosts do."

Grant gulped.

"Danfy is a *ghost*? And he lives on *this* train? And you've seen this ghost?" Christina asked.

"Well, no," Anna admitted, "but we've heard him several times!"

"And whenever that happens," Paul said, "it gets really cold!"

7

A SPRINKLE OF GOLD

A soft yellow light filtered into their sleeping compartment from the club car ahead of them.

It must be Mimi getting a head start on her train mystery, figured Christina. *At least I'm not the only one who can't sleep.*

She sat up and pulled the curtain open. The night sky was a brilliant explosion of stars. She leaned back and pulled her soft blanket up close to her chin. She watched the full moon follow their train. The gentle rocking of the car finally lulled Christina to sleep.

"Christina!" Grant whispered. He shook his sister awake.

"Huh? Grant, is that you?" Christina asked. The light in the adjacent club car was off. Even the moon hid. It was pitch-black in the car.

"Yeah, it's me. I heard something!" Grant whimpered.

"What did you hear?" Christina asked. She was sitting up now.

"It's hard to explain," he said, and climbed into Christina's bed.

"Was it human? Animal?" Christina asked.

"I think," Grant answered. He yawned.

"Well, which was it–human or animal?" Christina asked again.

"I'm not sure," he answered.

"This old train makes weird sounds–ones we're not used to," Christina said. "Maybe it was the train engineer stopping for water, OK? Grant?" she called.

Grant was sound asleep–in her bed!

How am I going to fall back to sleep now? Christina wondered to herself.

She remembered she kept a book in her backpack. She climbed down the ladder to get it. Gathering courage, she crossed the room and switched on the desk lamp. A soft glow filled the room. Christina stopped in her tracks.

Anna and Paul were gone! And their beds were already made!

"That's weird!" Christina mumbled. She reached inside her backpack to pull out her book. Something slipped out of the pages and fell to the floor. She reached down to pick up a small envelope sprinkled with gold glitter.

A gold-leafed **vignette** decorated the right edge of the envelope. Christina turned it over. It was sealed shut with a tiny braided string!

"Brrr! It's cold," Christina mumbled. She hugged herself.

EEEEH! EEEEH!

Christina froze.

EEEEH! EEEEH!

She switched off the lamp and dove under the desk.

A faint, blue glow appeared under the door. It moved back and forth. The glow grew longer and moved closer to Christina's hiding place. She pulled her legs in tighter. Her teeth began to chatter.

Just then, the dim, blue light disappeared.

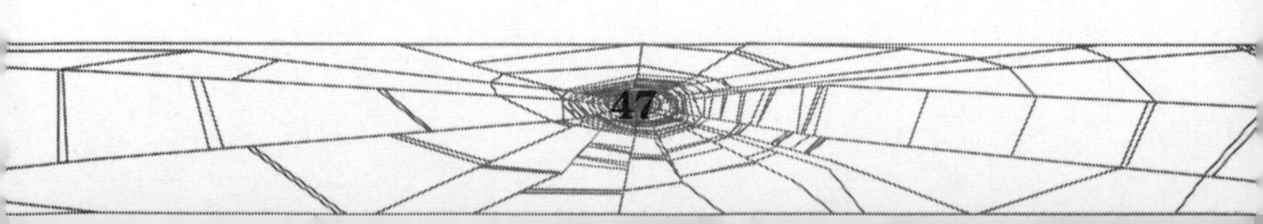

8
OVER AND OUT!

The morning sun filtered through a slit in the curtained window of the sleeper car, waking Grant with a start. He climbed down the ladder and surveyed the room.

"Christina?" he called out. No answer.

Grant noticed that Paul and Anna's beds were neatly made. *Maybe they went to eat breakfast without me!* he thought. Grant began to feel like he'd been abandoned.

Then he saw Christina curled up fast asleep under the desk by the door.

"Christina?" Grant whispered.

"Huh?" she mumbled. She sat up and rubbed the sleep from her eyes.

"Why are you asleep under the desk? And what's that in your hand?" Grant asked.

Christina opened her hand to reveal a golden envelope. "It's real?" shc whispered. "It wasn't a dream!"

"What wasn't a dream?" Grant asked, bewildered.

"Grant, do you remember telling me you heard a weird noise last night?" Christina asked.

"Oh, yeah!" he said.

"Well, I heard it, too!" she admitted. "But there was also a creepy blue light."

"Good thing you hid under the desk," he said. "What if it was Old Danfy making his nightly train rounds?"

KNOCK KNOCK KNOCK!

Christina and Grant jumped at the sound.

"Good morning!" sang Mimi as she slid the door open.

"Mimi!" they cried. "Good morning!"

"Did you two sleep well?" she asked.

"Uh huh," they said.

The delicious aroma of freshly baked biscuits and pancakes floated into their car.

"Good! Breakfast will be served in five minutes. You know, I feel more pampered on this train than I do in a four-star hotel!" she stated.

"Well, I'm starved!" Grant exclaimed.

Mimi chuckled. "See you soon, then!" She left, humming a familiar train tune. Grant got up to get dressed.

"Don't you want to hear about the envelope?" Christina asked.

"Oh, OK," he said.

Christina explained how the envelope fell out of her book.

Grant stared at the golden envelope, turned it over, and said, "So someone slipped it into your book when you weren't looking?"

Christina got goose bumps. "Must have!" she replied. "I also found these, one at the hotel and the other in Papa's luggage tag."

"They're shaped like puzzle pieces," Grant said.

"That's what I thought," Christina said.

Grant opened the envelope by unwinding the braided string. Inside was another golden puzzle piece. But this one had writing on it:

"A clue!?" Grant asked. "Why would someone leave you a clue?"

"Who knows?!" Christina replied. "I just wish that for once–just once–we could have a normal vacation, with no mystery to solve!"

"Well, technically, Christina, *you* found the clue," Grant said. "So..."

"So, nothing!" Christina exclaimed. "You heard that creepy sound last night. And that creepy sound and these puzzle clues might be related. So, *technically*, you're involved, too," she reasoned.

"Uh...I'm not really sure what you just said because, well, I can't think at all on an empty stomach. So..." Grant said.

"Fine! Oooh, you can be so annoying!" Christina complained. "By the way, where did Anna and Paul go last night?" she asked on their way to eat breakfast.

"Why would I know that?" Grant asked.

"Well, their beds were already made when you woke me up last night," she explained.

"I have *no* idea!" Grant exclaimed, shaking his head. "I don't understand why *anyone* would *ever* make their bed! You're just going to sleep in it the next day!"

"True," Christina agreed, smiling.

At breakfast, Paul and Anna admitted to having heard the scary noises.

"We went to sleep with Miss Tess," Anna said.

"Well, I don't get it!" Grant said. "If you left because you were scared, then why did you stay to make your beds first?" Grant asked.

"We didn't! Maybe Miss Tess did," Paul guessed, shrugging his shoulders.

"You just left us there with Old Danfy?" Grant asked.

"Oh!" Anna cried. "Paul took off and I followed. I wanted to go back for you, but I was too scared!"

"We're sorry! We won't do that again," they promised.

After breakfast, Grant and Paul struck out to explore on their own.

"The last time we heard Old Danfy," Paul told Grant, "was two weeks ago in Grandpa's private car. We found an old journal–"

"Wait, 'Grandpa's' car? Mr. Goodfellow is your grandfather?" Grant asked, surprised.

"Uh huh," Paul answered.

"And you found a journal?" Grant asked.

"Yeah, it had the initials JMG on the front and it was full of big, golden puzzle pieces!" Paul said.

Grant's mouth flew open. "Puzzle pieces?" he asked, startled.

"Yes! That's when Anna and I heard Old Danfy howling away," Paul said. "It scared us bad then, too, so we took off running!"

"Where is the journal now?" Grant asked.

"No idea," admitted Paul. "When Anna and I went back, the journal was gone!"

"...ant, you there?" Christina's voice screeched over the walkie talkie.

"Christina, hold the button down longer before you start talking," Grant instructed.

"Uh, OK! Grant, you there?" she repeated.

"No," Grant answered, smiling.

"Very funny! Mimi and Papa need you and Paul in the observation car ASAP," Christina relayed. "We're ten minutes from–"

"From where, Christina?" Grant asked.

"Ha! Just making sure you were listening!" she joked. "We're ten minutes–no, scratch that–Papa says nine minutes from the water stop in St. Louis. And just where are you, anyway?"

"Five minutes away! Tell Papa we'll be there in a jiffy!" Grant said.

"SQUAAAAKK! SQUAAAKK!"

"What was *that*?" Christina asked.

Grant answered, "You'll never believe this! Mr. Goodfellow has a pet parrot in his private car! Over and out!"

Then to Paul, Grant said, "We have to run–NOW!"

9

FALSE ALARM

Engineer Luke was tending to *The General* while Mimi, Papa, and the kids walked across the famous Eads Bridge in St. Louis, Missouri.

"What is that? It's huge!" Grant cried. His mouth gaped open as he pointed at a huge metal arch curving gracefully over the landscape.

"Do you mind, Grant? You're gonna catch a fly!" Christina warned.

Grant snapped his mouth shut. "You're just saying that because you don't know what that arch is!"

"Do too! It's just that your mouth is such a distraction!" Christina cried.

Paul and Anna giggled.

"OK, you two. Been cooped up in that train too long, I see," Papa said. "That, children, on the opposite bank of the river, is the Gateway Arch."

"Oh, my! It's windier than I thought it would be up here," Mimi cried. She tightened her red silk scarf over her short, blonde hair.

"The Gateway Arch," Mimi began, "is a monument to the westward expansion of the United States. It stands 630 feet, the highest man-made memorial in the country! That's twice as tall as the Statue of Liberty, by the way."

"And below the arch," Papa continued, "is the Museum of Westward Expansion. All of that sits on more than 90 acres of the Jefferson National Expansion Memorial."

"Is it a memorial for President Thomas Jefferson? Like in Washington, D.C., there's the Washington Monument and the Lincoln Memorial?" Christina wondered aloud.

"That's right, Christina," Papa said. "It was from here that Lewis and Clark set out on their famous expedition to explore and map out the West in 1804. It was Thomas Jefferson who ordered the expedition.

"But before exploration of the West was even possible, we had to own the land first," he continued. "The Louisiana Territory, a huge chunk of land from the Mississippi River all the way west to the Rocky Mountains, was owned by the French at the time."

Papa waved his arm across the landscape before them. "In 1803, Thomas Jefferson managed to buy the land for $15 million, or about three cents an acre!" he explained. "The sale, which was called the Louisiana Purchase, immediately doubled the size of the United States!"

"So after the Louisiana Purchase, Lewis and Clark left from here on that famous expedition?" Paul asked.

"That's right, Paul," Papa said.

"Luke just called," Mimi announced. "He says he's got business in St. Louis, and he's arranged a replacement for now."

Papa looked annoyed. "Is the train ready for departure?"

"Yes! Engineer Sam is waiting on us now," Mimi relayed.

"Good! We should be heading back then," Papa decided.

They followed Papa back across the bridge as the blue-green water of the Mississippi River sparkled beneath them. A white steamboat chugged lazily upstream.

Suddenly, the bridge shook!

"It's an earthquake!" Grant shouted and ran in circles. He smacked into Papa. His feet were still pumping when Papa lifted him high into the air.

"Grant, settle down!" Papa warned. "That wasn't an earthquake. It's a train crossing the lower deck of this bridge. We'll be crossing it soon ourselves on our trek to the West!"

10

TRAINS AND TRAILS

The engine was already rumbling as Mimi, Papa, and the kids rounded the corner of the station yard. Engineer Sam, the replacement, reached out of the cab to give Papa the go-ahead. He wore a black engineer's cap and a pair of dark sunglasses.

"All aboard!" Papa bellowed. To play it safe this time, he did a headcount. "...four, five, and Grant makes six passengers!"

The mid-morning sun angled through the crossbeams of the lower deck of the Eads Bridge. It had the effect of a light being switched on and off in the observation car, where the kids were enjoying slices of dark chocolate cake.

"Where are we headed next?" Grant asked. Creamy chocolate frosting formed a ring around his mouth.

"Glad you asked!" Papa said. "We'll make a brief stop in Independence, Missouri, on our way to Omaha, Nebraska."

Papa smoothed out the creases in his map. "This is Independence, Missouri," he said, pointing to the landlocked state nestled between Illinois and Kansas. "Independence has some interesting history, in addition to being home to my personal favorite president, Harry S. Truman.

"The Missouri River feeds the Mississippi River," Papa continued. "The town of Independence, Missouri, was built up where the two rivers meet."

"And during Westward Expansion," Mimi added, "Independence was where the Oregon Trail began."

"Oregon Trail?" wondered Grant. "But Independence is a city in Missouri. Why was it called the *Oregon* Trail?"

"That's because the trail ended in Oregon," Mimi explained.

"The Oregon Trail was the famous trail the pioneers took out west before the First

Transcontinental Railroad was built, right?" Christina asked.

"That's right," Mimi said. "Travelers would stop in Independence and restock their wagons with supplies before setting off."

"There's a photo in the observation car of a huge rock with the words 'Oregon Trail' under it," Anna said.

"That's Chimney Rock," Papa said. "That's further down the Oregon Trail, though, and unfortunately, not on our itinerary. It was a famous landmark for pioneers heading out West. It was pretty hard to miss!"

"And the California Trail branched off from the Oregon Trail in Idaho," Mimi said.

"People took the California Trail to get to California, right!?" Grant asked.

"That's right. Gold was discovered there in 1848. Tens of thousands of travelers flooded into California to strike it rich!" Papa said.

"Then, twenty years later," Mimi added, "the First Transcontinental Railroad was built. It instantly cut the travel time across the country from six months to a week."

"What I don't understand is why people would travel six months–you know, before train travel–to cross very dangerous territory. Weren't they happy where they were?" Christina asked.

"There were many reasons why people moved west," Mimi explained. "The fur traders used the trails to hunt. Immigrants left crowded eastern cities to find work. Others were looking for adventure. But probably the biggest reason was a chance to own land and start a new life."

"And don't forget about 'Manifest Destiny'," Papa added.

"Man what?" Grant asked.

"Manifest Destiny," repeated Papa. "It was the strong belief at the time that Americans should spread out across the North American continent–that it was their destiny!"

"Well, it's *my* destiny to get some more yummy cake!" Grant cried. He skipped over to the cart where Miss Tess had left second helpings. Then he saw it–another golden puzzle piece!

11

CAUGHT IN THE ACT!

"Do you think Miss Tess left this clue on the cake cart?" Grant whispered to Christina.

"Maybe! The question is why!" she whispered back.

Paul and Anna joined their friends at the cart. "Hey, want to go exploring?" Paul asked Grant.

Grant looked over at Christina. "Go on!" Christina urged. "Anna and I will stay here." The boys took off with lightning speed.

Christina glanced outside. The Gateway Arch was nowhere in sight. The Missouri landscape was changing from office buildings to farms. She leaned in and whispered, "Grant and I have been finding clues."

"Seriously, clues? You mean like in a mystery?" Anna asked.

"It does sound weird, I know!" Christina replied. "But someone's been leaving golden puzzle pieces around for us to find."

Anna's eyes widened. "Paul and I found golden puzzle pieces a couple of weeks ago in Grandpa's private car!"

"*Grandpa?*" Christina exclaimed. "Mr. Goodfellow is your grandfather?"

"Well, yes," Anna said, looking surprised. "That's why we're on the train. We wanted to ride it one last time before Grandpa sells it."

"Well, that makes sense!" Christina admitted. "Do you still have the golden puzzle pieces?"

"Actually, Old Danfy spooked us, so we ran!" admitted Anna. "They were stuffed inside a leather journal. When we went back, the journal and the puzzle pieces were gone!"

Their conversation was suddenly interrupted. "Christina, you there?" It was Grant on the walkie talkie. He was whispering. "Never mind, don't answer. Just listen!"

Christina swung her backpack around and fished out her walkie talkie.

Grant continued, "We're hiding in the wardrobe from someone. Don't worry. He doesn't know we're here. He's looking through Mr. Goodfellow's desk!"

A shiver ran up Christina's back.

"Grandpa's desk?" Anna said to Christina. "What would he want in there?"

"Grant and Paul are in trouble! Come on!" Christina cried. They took off running.

"Do you think the man boarded the train while Luke stopped for water in St. Louis?" Anna asked Christina.

"Probably. Wait! Get down!" Christina grabbed Anna's arm and yanked her to the floor.

They crawled on their hands and knees through the baggage car. They stopped at the door to the private car where their brothers were trapped.

"Let's look on the count of three!" Christina said. Anna nodded. "One, two, three!" Christina whispered. The girls peeked into the private car.

A tall man, with his back to the girls, was wearing a blue train uniform. He was rooting through the drawers of Mr. Goodfellow's desk. He opened the glass-encased bookcase and began pulling books out one by one.

Something about the guy seemed familiar to Christina, but she couldn't put her finger on it. She felt that what he was doing was **reprehensible.** She thought hard how to stop him.

"Mr. Good–your grandfather–has a parrot, right?" Christina whispered.

"Yes, but Miss Tess moved him to clean out his cage. He's probably still with her," Anna said.

"I have an idea!" Christina said. "SQUAAAK! SQUAAAK!" she screamed into the walkie talkie.

The man looked up. He scanned the room. "Who's there?" he cried.

"SQUAAAK! SQUAAAK!" Christina repeated.

The man dropped the book he was holding and backed into a thin manila file on the desk. It slapped the floor. He reached down to pick it up. SMACK! He bumped his head on the open drawer.

"OUCH!" he cried. The intruder grabbed the file and slipped out onto the caboose.

"What do we do now?" Anna asked.

"Go get our brothers!" Christina squealed.

Just as the girls swung the closet doors open, Grant sprung out of the closet and pinned Christina to the floor.

"Wow, kung fu master! Great move! Too bad it's just your sister!" Paul kidded and laughed out loud.

"Get off me!" Christina yelled. "He's getting away!"

They scrambled to look out onto the caboose.

"Is he really going to jump?" Christina asked, alarmed. The man was sitting on the rail with his legs dangling over the side. They watched in horror as he jumped off the back of the slow-moving train.

"Did you see where he went?" Grant asked frantically.

Paul joked, "It's like one of those horror movies, where the guy disappears and everyone thinks he's gone for good, but then later he pops up out of nowhere!"

"RAAAAA!" Grant roared behind Paul. Paul screamed and chased Grant around the room.

The man crouched low on the ledge of the caboose, waiting patiently for the kids to leave.

12
A PUZZLING WILL

Anna trudged over to the desk and plopped down in the leather swivel chair. "Why would someone want to steal from Grandpa?" she wondered aloud. "First, Grandpa's about to lose his ranch in Texas, which has been in the family for generations! And now this!" Anna looked ready to cry.

"Oh, Anna, Paul, I didn't know!" Christina said sympathetically.

She leaned down to return the books to the shelf. "Huh?" Christina murmured. "This feels too light to be a book." She read the title on the spine. "*The Complete Works of William Shakespeare: Plays and Poetry.*"

"Shake's spear?" Grant said. "Shake's spear shook! Shake's spear shook! Bet you can't say that five times fast!" he joked, pointing to a spear hanging on the wall above the door.

Ignoring Grant, Anna asked Christina, "You think it might be hollow?"

Christina giggled at Grant's play on words and handed Anna the book.

Anna's hand was visibly shaking when she lifted the cover. Inside was a royal-blue velvet lining with the impression of a key in its center.

"It's supposed to hide a key!" Anna said.

"A key to what?" Paul wondered aloud. Anna and the others shrugged.

Anna said, "Paul, remember when we found the journal filled with golden puzzle pieces?"

Paul nodded. "Yeah, Grant and I were just talking about that."

"Well, did he tell you someone's been leaving them around for Christina and Grant to find?" Anna asked.

"They're *what*?" Paul asked incredulously.

"It's true," Grant said.

"And I have a sneaking suspicion they want us to figure out what the puzzle pieces mean!" Christina said.

"If they want you to figure out what they mean, why don't they just ask you for help?" Paul asked.

"I don't know," Christina answered.

Just then, something slapped the window of the private car.

"It's a piece of paper!" Grant exclaimed.

"Grab it before it blows away!" Christina cried.

Grant opened the door and peeled the paper off the window. He handed the paper to Anna.

"Where did *that* come from?" Paul asked.

"The thief probably dropped it before he made his getaway!" Grant guessed.

"What does it say?" Christina asked.

Anna scanned the yellowing paper. Her face blanched. "It's a will dated October 5, 1941," she whispered.

"Well, what does it say?" Paul urged.

"It's not written in English," Anna said.

"May I?" Christina asked, holding out her hand. Her eyes grew wide. "But, Anna, this is English!"

Christina scanned the walls of the private car. She avoided looking at the bear. "Over here!" she shouted.

Christina held the will up to a gold-leaf framed mirror. The kids crowded around while she read the reversed letters in the mirror:

To my grandson, whom I have yet to meet due to my grave illness, I bequeath a golden key.

This grandson, whose name is John Lee Goodfellow, born the 27th day of August in the year 1941, shall use this golden key to uncover a fortune amassed at the peak of my career.

It is my hope that this fortune will be used to continue my legacy and that of our ancestors for many generations to come.

The mystery which surrounds the location of this fortune is not an accident. The golden key is only the beginning.

"The golden key?" Christina whispered. "Do you think it's talking about the key from the book?"

"That's what I was thinking," Grant exclaimed.

Christina handed the will back to Anna.

"So, it's Grandpa's *grandpa's* will!" Anna cried.

"So, it's not your grandfather's, and not your great-grandfather's, but your great-great-grandfather's will?" Grant asked.

"Exactly! See, it says here that this will was drawn up for John Marshall Goodfellow," Anna said.

"Well, that explains who the journal belonged to!" Grant said, surprising everyone.

"How do you know that?" Paul asked.

"JMG! You told me the letters inscribed on the cover of the journal were JMG–John Marshall Goodfellow!" Grant explained.

"Hmm, I guess you're right!" Paul said.

"Gosh! If Grandpa finds the treasure, he won't lose the land!" Anna exclaimed. "Or the train! I imagine this train is part of the Goodfellow legacy that our great-great-grandpa was talking about in his will."

"Grandpa probably doesn't even know the will exists!" Paul said.

"But, wait a second," Grant said. "How do we know that the key and the golden puzzle pieces have anything to do with each other? I mean, the key–wherever it is–may unlock some other mystery."

"That's a good point, Grant," Christina said. "And I think I have the answer." She handed the golden envelope to Anna.

"This is really pretty, Christina!" Anna said. She unwound the braided string and read the puzzle-shaped clue, "Puzzled yet? The day's first light reveals all!"

Anna stared hard at the puzzle piece. "The handwriting–it's the same as in the will!" she exclaimed. She turned the clue over. On the back, in very small letters were the initials:

JMG

"And here are his initials again!" Anna said, looking up at Christina.

"So there's the link!" Christina said.

Paul asked, "What do we do now?"

"We wait!" Christina advised.

The man waiting out of sight was relieved when the kids finally left. The heat rising from the track was becoming truly unbearable!

13
A DETOUR WORTH TAKING!

"Christina, didn't anyone teach you that reading at the table is rude?" Grant asked.

"Grant, didn't anyone teach you that talking with your mouth full is rude?" Christina countered. "And besides, I'm reading something educational. I found this book about the Pony Express in Mr. Goodfellow's library."

"The Pony Express?" Grant asked. "What's that?"

Christina explained, "Before 1860, information took forever to get across the country. For example, it was about a year before people in the East found out about the gold discovery in California in 1848!

"So, in 1860," Christina continued, "nine years before the First Transcontinental

Railroad linked the East and the West, the Pony Express was started."

"Was it a way to deliver the news across the country?" Grant asked.

"Probably the news too, but mostly the mail," Christina explained. "A relay of brave Pony Express riders rode between 75 and 100 miles each, stopping to change horses at relay stations about every 10 to 15 miles. The westbound route started in St. Joseph, Missouri, and ended in San Francisco, California. The eastbound route went the opposite direction–from California to Missouri."

"It sounds like the relay races at school. But instead of a baton, the riders would pass mailbags to a new rider!" Grant said.

Just then, Anna cried, "Christina, Grant, come quick! You're not going to believe this!"

Christina put down her book and sprinted to the window. Racing alongside the train was a herd of wild, black-and-white splotched pinto horses.

"Awesome! There must be fifty of them!" cried Grant.

"They're beautiful!" Anna exclaimed. "They're close enough to touch!"

The horses pulled ahead, leaving a trail of thick dust in their wake.

"We have to warn Papa!" Christina cried. "They might get hit if they try to cross in front of us!" The children raced to the engine cab.

"Papa!" Grant exclaimed, trying to catch his breath. "Wild horses!" He pointed to the approaching herd to their left.

"Well, would you take a look at that!" Papa exclaimed.

A man of about sixty, sporting a white beard and dark sunglasses, was fiddling with valves and checking gauges. "That is a rare sight indeed," he said, nodding in the direction of the herd. "You must be Grant," he said.

"Are you Engineer Sam?" Grant asked.

"That I am! Ever sounded a whistle before?" Sam asked. "You can tell a lot about a man by his whistle."

Grant gestured to the pull cord. "May I?" he asked.

“Be my guest!” Engineer Sam said.

Grant pulled the cord, sounding the whistle in his own unique way. TOOT! TOOT! TOOT! TOOT! TOOT!

“Not bad at all!” Engineer Sam said.

“The horses!” Christina cried. “They’re leaving!” They veered off to the left and disappeared in a cloud of dust.

Just then, Mimi climbed into the cab. She snapped her cell phone shut. “I just got a call from Luke!” she said, out of breath.

“Is he still in St. Louis?” Papa asked.

“Yes, he is,” she said.

“Why did he call?” Papa asked.

“To warn us! There are tornado sightings all up and down our Kansas route. He’s already called ahead to reroute the train in Omaha, Nebraska,” she explained.

The countryside was being replaced by signs of civilization: a house here, a gas station there. Their steam train drew curious stares from people along the route. Papa sounded the whistle. TOOT! TOOT! Children cheered and waved.

"Look, there's the Omaha, Nebraska, Union Station. And they're expecting us!" Papa exclaimed. A man in a blue uniform and black cap directed them to a side rail at the switching yard, where Papa expertly pulled in and left the engine idling.

"We're not stopping here, are we?" Grant asked.

"The train needs oil and water, Grant," Papa explained. "We certainly don't want to get stuck out in the middle of Nebraska!"

"Between you and me, Papa, I'd rather get stuck out in the middle of Nebraska than get sucked up and spit out by a giant tornado!" Grant admitted.

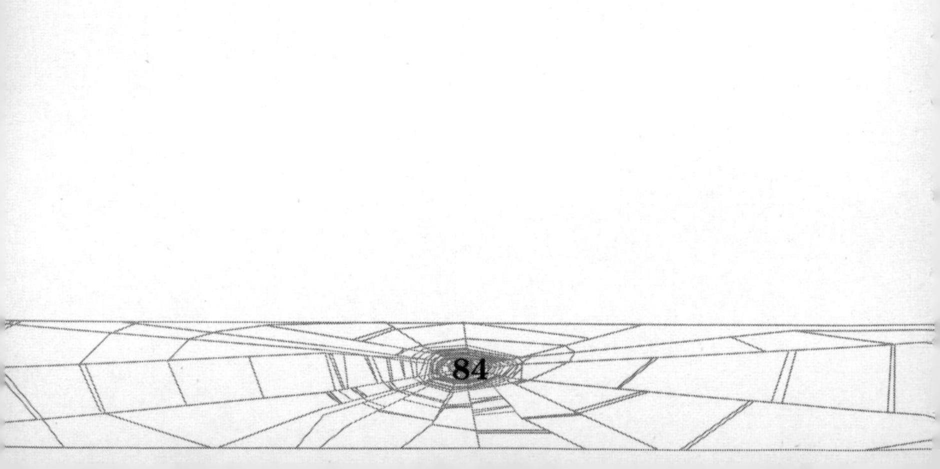

14
CRASH LANDING!

"I'll leave this train on one condition," Grant said.

"What's that?" Christina asked.

"If a tornado does hit, you have to promise that we'll come right back!" Grant insisted.

"This train may not be the safest place to be in a tornado, Grant," Christina explained. "Anyway, that's for Mimi and Papa to decide, not me."

Grant nodded. "I guess."

"Downtown Omaha is home to the Union Pacific Railroad Historical Museum," Mimi announced. "The museum has quite the train collection–artifacts dating back from the pioneer days, even before the First Transcontinental Railroad linked America."

"And for the diehard train fan," Papa explained, "there are displays documenting the hardships the rail builders endured, along with stories of train robberies and the fate of those infamous outlaws."

"I'm in!" Grant exclaimed.

"You had me at 'train robberies'!" Paul said. "And 'outlaws'!"

"Gosh, Christina, I can't believe you were afraid of a little old tornado!" Grant kidded.

"What? I wasn't afraid–oh, I'll get you for that!" Christina shouted. She chased her brother out of the train and onto the platform. "Grant! Wait! Stop!" she shouted, but it was too late!

CRASH! Grant ran right into a man wearing a blue uniform and a black cap. The man's cap was knocked right off his head. It landed on the tracks below.

The man covered his forehead with his gloved hand and scooted passed Grant, accidentally knocking him to the floor.

"Oh, sorry, I–" he murmured and limped off.

"Gosh, Grant, you really hurt him! Did you see that gash on his forehead?" Paul asked.

Grant stood up and dusted himself off. "I didn't touch his head!" he said.

"It's true, Paul," Christina said, defending her brother. She scanned the station platform. "Look, there's his bloody handkerchief!"

"Who puts a handkerchief on a gash like that? It must have just happened!" Paul said.

"That was weird! Should we get it?" Anna asked.

"The handkerchief?" Paul asked, surprised. Anna shook her head.

"What? The cap? And risk getting hit by a train? No way!" Grant refused.

"I've got it!" shouted a stocky, red-headed station worker, grabbing the hat.

"They really need to make these poles longer!" he complained. "I can't tell you how many caps I pull off this track every day! Kids bug their parents for a train engineer's cap, and the minute they put it on, it blows right off their head!" he exclaimed with a huff.

He turned to Christina. “Take it!” he snarled. “And tell your brother, or whoever that is, to be more careful!” the stocky man warned and stomped away.

Christina looked at the cap in her hand. “Huh!?” she murmured and smiled. She slipped the cap into her backpack and joined Mimi and Papa as they exited *The General* on their way to the museum.

The train began to ease slowly down the track. “The train!” exclaimed Grant, “Someone’s stealing it!”

“Grant, this is where we get off, that’s all. *The General* is being moved to an area equipped to handle old steam trains,” Papa explained. “They’ll take good care of it!”

I hope so, Christina thought. *I want to find out what’s really going on aboard that train!*

15
YOU'VE GOT MAIL!

Dark clouds pushed the setting sun over the horizon.

"Engineer Sam called," Mimi reported. "*The General* is ready and waiting."

"And right in the nick of time, too!" Papa bellowed. "The sky looks to be brewing trouble!"

"What kind of trouble?" Grant asked. "The tornado kind?"

"Let's not stick around to find out!" Papa exclaimed.

The General headed west, a planned detour from their original plan to travel southwest into Kansas, where a number of tornadoes were reportedly sighted.

"Mimi, look!" Christina cried. "The windows! They're shaking!"

"We should get to the dining car quickly, then!" Mimi cried. "We really don't want to car-hop in the rain!"

The dining car was filled with the aroma of carefully prepared dishes. Candles glowed at each table.

"Thank you for this lovely meal, Miss Tess," Mimi said. "It was delicious!"

"Yes, thank you!" everyone shouted. Miss Tess beamed.

While Mimi waited for her dessert and coffee to go, she asked the kids, "What did you think of the museum?"

"I liked the miniature train displays and the stories about the train robbers," Paul said.

"I liked the displays," Anna confided. "They helped me understand how the new railroad made life so much better for so many people."

"I liked learning how President Lincoln supported the idea of a transcontinental railroad in the first place," Christina said. "And because of that, the West became developed and so did the United States."

Mimi nodded. "And what about you, Grant?" she asked.

"I liked the old stuff," said Grant, "like the old tickets and guns and train schedules and photos of the workers. The museum helped me believe that all of that history really happened."

"I'm glad you all learned something today," Mimi said with a warm smile. "I did, too! I'll be in the observation car writing, if you need me."

Suddenly, the sky cracked and the train shook.

"On second thought," Mimi said, "I think we'll all go to the observation car." Then to Miss Tess, "Where can I find clean linens? It looks like we may have to sleep in the observation car tonight!"

"Right this way!" Miss Tess answered.

"Mimi?" Christina said.

"I'd feel better if you stayed put. Don't let anyone leave the car, OK?" Mimi implored.

"OK, I won't," Christina promised.

When they were alone, Christina pulled the black cap out of her backpack.

"You kept it?" Grant asked, looking amused.

"Look at what's inside!" Christina said.

"No way!" Grant said. "More golden puzzle clues!"

"Wait!" Anna exclaimed. "They were in his cap?"

Christina nodded. She pulled all of the clues out and spread them out on the table. The kids fit the pieces together.

"We're still missing a few," Paul observed.

"I've been thinking," Grant began slowly. "How is it possible that of all the people on that train platform, I run into the one person with clues in his cap?"

The car went silent. Even the wind died down.

"Do you think that guy ran into you, and not the other way around?" Anna asked suddenly.

"Either that, or it's the biggest coincidence ever!" Paul said.

"What do you remember about the guy?" Christina asked.

She made a list.

1. *blue uniform,*
   black cap
2. *cut on forehead*
3. *had a limp*
4. *left his cap with the clues*

"You know, that thief guy hit his head pretty hard on the desk drawer," Christina said.

"Do you think it's the same guy?" asked Grant.

"It has to be!" Anna decided. "He left the cap, probably so we wouldn't get a good look at his face."

Christina rolled up the incomplete puzzle and slipped it into her backpack. "Actually," she said, "I think he's been trailing us for awhile–at least since the hotel."

"Really?" Grant said.

"There was a guy in the hall where I found the first clue. He seemed really nervous. In fact, he ran into the wall," Christina said. "If it is the same guy, maybe that's how he got the limp."

Just then, Mimi and Miss Tess entered the dining car, balancing blankets and pillows up to their eyes. Grant and Paul ran to help them.

Mimi peered out the window and said, "Well, it looks like we outran the storm." The sky had opened up. A wash of pink and purple pastels sprung up from the horizon. But suddenly, they heard the earth pound with a rhythmic beat.

"What is that?" Mimi asked.

"It's a horse!" Christina said.

"The mail is here!" Anna announced. "Come on! It's how Grandpa gets his mail!"

Anna waved to the woman on horseback. She was wearing a cowboy hat, blue jeans, and silver spurs on her cowboy boots. Attached to her saddle was a leather mailbag.

The children raced ahead to the observation car and opened the door. Thick shrubs sprung in clumps from the wet earth.

"OK, move back everyone!" Paul yelled.

The woman slowed her horse to a trot and tossed the buckled mailbag through the open door. Anna picked it up and emptied the mail onto a table.

"Here, Paul," Anna said, tossing him the empty mailbag. Paul hurled the bag out the door. The woman caught it, waved, and raced off.

"Mimi, the Pony Express came by!" Grant shouted, when Mimi entered the car. "Well, it wasn't the real Pony Express, but did you see?"

"Yes, I did!" Mimi said. She and Miss Tess retreated to the dining car for some coffee.

"Christina," Anna said, "you've got mail!"

The envelope was thick. On the address line, in scrawled handwriting, it read,

Christina grabbed the envelope to see who sent it, but it showed no return address. She reached inside the envelope and pulled out several individually wrapped golden puzzle pieces!

"They know my name!" Christina exclaimed.

16

A TAME SIX INCHES

"Christina, you awake?" It was Grant.

Christina sat up and yawned. "I am now! You didn't hear those scary noises again, did you?" she cried.

"No, nothing like that!" Grant said. "The train–it's stopped!"

"Where do you think we are?" Christina asked, rubbing her eyes.

"Somewhere in Nebraska!" said Anna.

"Anna, you're awake, too?" Christina asked her friend.

"I am, too," Paul said.

Everyone was already dressed.

Christina climbed down the ladder. "I'll be back in a second," she said. Christina came out of the bathroom dressed in a pair of jeans and a T-shirt.

"Look outside!" Grant urged Christina when she rejoined them.

"A fire!" Christina exclaimed.

"A campsite," Grant corrected.

Christina peered out the window. "There's a covered wagon! And that must be Chimney Rock!"

Towering above the flat Nebraska skyline stood a mound of rock, with a rocky finger jutting up from its summit like a chimney.

"Wow!" Christina exclaimed. "I guess that famous pioneer landmark ended up on the itinerary after all!" she said, laughing.

KNOCK KNOCK KNOCK! It was Mimi. "Good! You're awake–and dressed! Why am I not surprised?" she said.

Mimi led the crew outside. "Go on! We thought you might need a little adventure after being cooped up for so long on the train."

"Hey, what's that yummy smell?" Grant asked, sniffing the air.

"Go find out!" Mimi urged.

A figure moved about the campfire, which had been reduced to a tame six inches.

"Miss Tess, is that you?" Anna called.

"It is indeed, children!" Miss Tess answered. "Come now! Have some biscuits and hot cocoa!"

A warm, heavy breeze swept the worn Nebraska prairie. Chimney Rock loomed large in the distance. They gathered around what Miss Tess called a Dutch oven, a black, iron pot that balanced on a tripod over the open flames.

"Air blows under the pot, you see, and these hot rocks placed on top of the lid help to evenly cook the biscuits," Miss Tess explained. She handed each of the kids a warm biscuit wrapped in a red-and-white checkered napkin.

"This is so fun!" Christina exclaimed. "I feel like we're pioneers of the Old West!"

"I've wanted to do this since I was a little girl," Miss Tess confessed. For a split second, Christina pictured Miss Tess as a young girl with pink cheeks and flowing raven hair.

"Pioneers moving out west faced many challenges," Miss Tess began, "from the weather to wild animals, and even though there were many friendly Indian tribes, there were some that weren't.

"Pioneer families traveled single-file in caravans called wagon trains," she continued. "They weren't really trains; the long line of covered wagons only looked like trains."

"How did they keep safe while they traveled?" Christina asked.

"There was safety in numbers," Miss Tess explained. "When they stopped for the night, the wagon train would form a large, tight circle. The kids were only allowed to play inside the circle."

Anna asked, "With so many families to look after, how far could they travel in one day?"

"Ten to fifteen miles on a good day," she answered.

"But how did they know where to go?" Christina asked.

"Scouts, usually former fur traders, knew the area like the back of their hands," Miss Tess replied. "They would advise the captain about which rivers to cross and what mountain passes were the safest."

Miss Tess ambled over to the covered wagon. One of its mahogany wheels had splintered and cracked decades ago, causing the abandoned wagon to lean far to one side. The torn cover flapped in the wind.

"Hello there, good folk!" It was Grant. Paul waved from his perch next to him on the covered wagon's weathered seat. "We're taking this here trail to California to seek our fortune! Care to join us in our trusty covered wagon?"

A kerosene lantern hung from a rusty hook where they sat. Its flame burned fiercely.

Miss Tess laughed. "Boys, it looks like your oxen have gone on without you! Now, climb on down from there and have a cup of hot cocoa," she said warmly.

17
IN TWO PLACES AT ONCE?

From the campsite, the entire train was visible, from the engine to the caboose.

"Look!" Christina whispered and pointed. "Old Danfy?"

A dim, blue light danced through the train cars. It moved gingerly from car to car, and then stopped abruptly. A light switched on!

"That's no ghost!" Anna whispered to Christina.

"Ghosts don't need light!" said Christina.

"Come on!" Anna said.

"We can't just leave Miss Tess. It's about to rain!" Christina reasoned.

"Miss Tess, can we take anything back to the train for you?" Anna asked.

"Oh, yes, would you?" Miss Tess replied. "Can you two manage this plastic tub with the heavy pots and pans?"

"Sure!" Christina said. The girls lifted the heavy tub and marched awkwardly towards the train.

"Mimi, Papa!" Christina called.

"We were just coming to get you!" cried Mimi.

Papa bellowed, "The storm's heading our way with a fury!"

Just then, lightning split the sky. Thunder roared. The girls struggled to move faster with their heavy load. For a split second, the silhouette of a person was cast on the curtain of the private car. Then the light went out!

"If Engineer Sam is in the engine cab..." Anna said, pointing to the lighted engine cab.

"...then who was that in the private car?" finished Christina. She shuddered.

Papa shouted, "I'll shovel dirt onto the flames, Grant. You and Paul ..."

The wind took the rest of the conversation somewhere else.

"Run!" Mimi hollered. She came up fast behind the girls.

Rain fell in sheets, drumming the plastic lid of the tub. And just ahead of them, the engine roared to life! The dim, blue light reappeared, retracing its path all the way back to the observation car, where it disappeared. POOF!

"Papa!" Grant yelled above the din of the storm. "My shoe! It's stuck in the mud!"

"Just leave it!" Papa shouted. "We're gonna get fried like chickens out here!"

Once safely inside, Papa did another headcount. "We'll be heading south tonight, towards Denver," he announced. "No one is to car-hop this evening. It's way too dangerous with the wind and rain. Is that understood?" he asked.

"Yes, sir," the kids promised.

Mimi stifled a yawn and spoke, "We're sleeping here in the observation car tonight!"

"Mimi," Christina asked quietly, "is Engineer Sam the only other person, besides Miss Tess, working on the train?"

"Uh huh," Mimi answered. She was busy spreading out the blankets and adjusting the pillows in the makeshift bedroom. "Why do you ask?"

"Outside, Anna and I thought we saw someone walking around in the private car," Christina explained.

"Isn't that where Petey, the parrot, usually stays?" Mimi asked. "Engineer Sam said something about returning him to the private car."

"Well, maybe that's who we saw!" Christina said. But deep down, Christina knew it was impossible to be in two places at once.

18

DREAMING IN POETRY!

Christina was glad when the storm passed. Puffy gray clouds sprinkled the night sky.

"You're going to tear it!" It was Grant.

"Grant, wake up," Christina whispered. "You're sleep-talking!"

"I was sleep-talking? Is that even a word?" Grant mumbled.

"If it's not, it should be," Christina said.

"I had the weirdest dream!" he cried.

"Shhh! You have to keep your voice down!" Christina warned.

"Mr. Goodfellow's parrot told me the same thing in my dream," Grant whispered.

"Huh?" Christina murmured.

"There was a key, too!" he said. "It was floating above me. Petey had a golden puzzle piece in his beak. I thought if I didn't get it back, we'd never solve the mystery!"

"Grant, you were just dreaming," Christina said. "Try to get some sleep, OK?"

After a minute or two, Christina could hear her brother's light snoring. She fell asleep when her head hit the pillow. She felt safe with Mimi nearby.

The tired oxen pulled the covered wagons,
Along a dusty trail!
It looked to her much like,
A wagon train setting sail!

The wheel got stuck,
Where many had stood the test!
She set her oxen free,
And carried all the rest!

A horse galloped by,
Kicking up dust!
The dust turned to golden confetti,
And blew away in a gust!

He wore a black cap,
And mounted his trusty steed!
And there just above his eye,
Was a gash–could it be?–for a very bad deed!

Christina woke with a start. Her heart was beating fast. *Did I just dream in poetry?* she wondered to herself.

"Grant?" she whispered. He was gone! "Anna, Paul!" Christina whispered. She shook her friends awake.

"What's wrong?" they asked, alarmed.

"I can't find Grant," Christina cried. "We have to find him!"

Paul shot up. "OK!" he agreed.

"Of course!" Anna replied.

They tiptoed out of the observation car. Once inside the dining car, they took off running.

"I see him!" Christina wailed. "There, in the club car!"

Grant was trudging along very slowly. "Open the door!" Christina cried.

"I'm trying," Paul grunted. "The...door...won't...budge!"

WHOOOOSH! It slid open.

"OK, now the other one!" Anna urged. It opened easily.

"There!" Anna shouted. Grant was opening the door to the sleeper car. "Grant! Stop!" she yelled.

"He's not stopping!" cried Christina. "Catch the door before it closes!"

"There he is, in the private car! He's heading for the caboose!" Paul warned.

Christina slipped open the door to the private car and bravely dodged the bear. "Grant! Stop!" she commanded.

When he didn't stop, Christina said, "This is for your own good, Grant!" She sprinted to the end of the car and tackled her brother mid-air. They fell to the floor with a THUD!

Grant sat up. He rubbed his eyes and then his head.

"How did I get in here?" Grant asked. "Ouch! My head hurts!"

"Dude," Paul said, "you were sleepwalking!"

"Christina had to tackle you before you went out onto the caboose!" Anna exclaimed.

"Whoa! I was? She did? That explains why I'm here and why my head hurts," Grant said.

"SQUAAAK! Golden key! SQUAAAK!"

"Petey!" Paul shouted, carefully removing the satin cover from the parrot cage. "Did we wake you?"

"When did you get back?" Anna asked Petey, as she gently tapped the cage.

"Engineer Sam brought him back here. Mimi told me," Christina said.

"But how is that possible?" Paul said. "I brought Petey back here after dinner. Miss Tess asked me to."

"If Engineer Sam didn't come back here with Petey, why *did* he come back here?" Anna asked.

"Maybe it wasn't Engineer Sam we saw in the window," Christina suggested.

"But you just said–" Anna began. "Oh! So Engineer Sam started the train, like we thought, and–"

"Someone else–" Christina began.

"Like that thief guy?" Anna suggested. "You know, we never really checked to see if he got off."

Suddenly, the track lighting that ran along the ceiling of the car began to flicker on and off. Then it went out completely!

19
SHADOWS IN THE DIRT

"Quick, Anna, switch on the desk lamp!" cried Paul. Anna crawled to the desk. She felt around for the lamp and pulled on the chain. "It's not working!" she cried.

"Try again," Paul suggested.

She felt for the bulb and froze. "The bulb–it's gone!" she whimpered.

"I'll check the desk," Christina offered. "No light bulbs!" she announced. "But I found a lantern!" She switched on the small, portable lantern. The room glowed blue.

"SQUAAAK! Golden key! SQUAAAK!" It was Petey.

The kids circled the cage.

"What do you have there, Petey?" Anna asked, peering into the cage.

Petey pulled at the newspaper lining the bottom of his cage.

"SQUAAAK! Golden key! SQUAAAK!"

Anna reached into Petey's cage and lifted the newspaper lining. "It's a golden key!" she exclaimed.

"Is that the golden key from your great-great-great, um? I mean great-great...?" Grant mumbled. "Gosh, Christina, did you really have to tackle me so hard?" he said rubbing his head again.

Just then, Petey dodged Anna's hand and flew around the room.

"This is what happened in my dream! Tell me I'm still dreaming!" Grant cried.

Petey perched on top of the gold-leaf framed mirror and pecked at it. "SQUAAAK! Golden key! SQUAAAK!"

"Anna, the key!" Paul cried. Anna handed Paul the key.

Petey hopped off the mirror and onto Paul's right shoulder. The bird turned awkwardly to face the mirror.

"I'm a pirate!" Paul kidded, making faces in the mirror. "This is Petey, my trusty parrot! I've searched high and low for me treasure. Have ya seen it?"

Petey pecked Paul hard on the cheek. "Ouch!" Paul eyed the parrot in the mirror.

"Don't you see?" Grant said. "He wants us to open the mirror, where there will be an old safe. And inside the safe, that's where we'll find the rest of the golden puzzle pieces. Then, we can solve this mystery once and for all!"

When the mirror opened and a safe appeared, Grant nearly fell over backwards onto the floor.

"But I was only kidding!" Grant exclaimed.

"Well, let's hope your prediction about the puzzle pieces is true, too!" Christina said.

Paul inserted the key into the safe. CLICK!

"It opened!" everyone cheered.

"Here's the journal," Paul said, "and one, two, three, four, and five puzzle pieces!" By the light of the lantern, he closed the safe and put Petey back in his cage.

"Good work, ol' boy," Paul whispered. He slipped the golden key back under the cage liner.

EEEEH! EEEEH! The room turned cold in seconds.

"Oh, no! Not again," Christina cried. She dropped the lantern. POP! The room went dark.

"Let's get out of here!" Grant shouted. Everyone scrambled to get out at the same time.

"I can't see the nose on my own face!" Christina cried.

"The journal! Who has the journal?" Anna cried.

"I put it on the desk," Paul answered. "I'll find it!"

"Ouch, you stepped on my hand!" Anna yelled.

"Sorry!" Paul apologized.

"A light! Someone's in the baggage room!" Grant whispered.

The kids grew quiet. The door slid open, and a bright light shone down on them. The kids instinctively covered their heads.

"Children?" It was Mimi's voice. "What are you doing here in the middle of the night in the dark?" she asked them.

"Mimi!" the children cried and ran to her.

"Ooh! It's chilly in here!" she said, shivering. "I woke up to find you all gone. I thought you might have moved to your beds."

"Grant was sleepwalking, and–it's a long story, Mimi," Christina said.

"We'll be pulling into the Denver Union Station in a few hours," Mimi said. "Your beds might be more comfortable than the benches in the observation car."

After they were alone in their sleeper car, Paul said, "The journal! I never got the journal!"

Christina looked out the window. The sun was already popping up over the horizon, casting weird shadows on the landscape outside. She turned around.

Christina's eyes grew wide! "Look, he's on the roof!"

The kids ran to the window. "See his shadow in the dirt? He's on the roof!" she repeated.

Grant ran to the door and slid it open.

"Grant!" cried Christina. "No way! Don't you dare!"

"Sorry, huh, what did you say?" Grant said, grinning. He slid the door closed behind him. Christina followed him out the door.

"Paul, not you, too?" Anna shouted.

Paul shrugged and disappeared up the ladder. Anna watched in horror as the silhouette of her brother and friends crept closer to the man waving the journal high in the air.

Anna raced to the end of the private car. *Maybe I'll be able to cut him off!* she thought. She climbed up the ladder.

"Watch it!" the man shouted. She threw her arm up to keep from getting kicked.

The man leaped over Anna and just barely cleared the gap between the train cars. He landed squarely on his feet and stood up, trying to balance on the uneven roof of the caboose.

"Mister! Duck!" Christina shouted.

The man turned and saw the tunnel closing in on him! He belly-flopped onto the roof of the train, but lost his grip on the journal. It skidded towards Anna.

"Anna, the journal!" Christina shouted.

"I can't reach the caboose ladder, Christina," Anna cried. "It's too far!"

Christina ducked low and ran as fast as she could. The tunnel was getting darker by the second. She jumped across the gap and landed safely on the other side.

"Christina!" Anna cried. "Grab it, quick!"

The man scrambled quickly towards the journal. He reached out to grab it.

TOOT TOOT!

The whistle blew so loud, the man covered his ears. Christina saw her chance and took it! She dove onto the journal, smacking her elbows on the roof.

"I got it!" Christina cheered.

The tunnel went pitch black.

"Hang on, everyone!" Christina yelled.

When the train exited the tunnel into the bright sun, the outline of the Denver skyline sprang into view.

"The guy–he's gone!" Grant exclaimed.

20

ASTRONAUTS AIN'T GOLD DIGGERS!

The next morning, the kids raced through breakfast, annoying Miss Tess to no end. “Children, you’re going to choke on your pancakes! Slow down and chew!” she said.

“The train–it’s slowing down! See you later, Miss Tess. Thanks for breakfast!” Grant cried.

The kids raced to the front, where Mimi led them out of the train and into a cab that took them to the Denver Union Station, while the train got serviced at the temporary train station.

Just in front of the old station building was a huge expanse of leveled land dotted with cranes, parked construction trucks, and mounds of dirt. A car honked in the distance.

"What happened to the station?" Grant asked.

"This, Grant, is the future of rail stations in the United States," Papa said, waving his arm out in front of him.

"This?" Grant asked.

"Well, not this, but in fewer than five years, this place will be completely transformed into a modern, state-of-the-art facility, meeting the needs of train and bus commuters alike," Papa explained.

"In my research, I came across some renderings of the plans for the station," said Mimi. "If the new light and heavy rails and the underground bus station are the only things built, the station will still be very impressive."

"What else do they plan to build, Mimi?" Christina asked, fascinated.

"Imagine a place where you'd want to take your family to spend the entire day," Mimi challenged.

"Wow!" exclaimed Grant. "Nope, I don't see it."

Mimi turned Grant to face the historic Union Station building. "Picture this," she said, "restaurants, cafés, lots of green space, an open area for concerts, fountains, and even a shady area to the left with a fountain of pop-up water jets that children can actually run through during the hot summer months," Mimi said.

"That would be so fun!" Grant exclaimed.

"The people of Denver will probably feel just as proud of their new station as the residents of Washington, D.C., did over one hundred years ago when that station was built," Christina said.

Mimi smiled. "I think you're right!" She and Papa walked arm-in-arm, ahead of the kids.

Christina was proud that she lived in a country that honored the past and looked to the future. She turned to look at the old station–at its arches, clock, and bright letters that spelled 'UNION STATION TRAVEL *by* TRAIN' across the top.

"The message!" Christina cried.

"Where?" Grant asked, squinting his bright blue eyes.

"No, we have to read the message in the envelope again! That's the key to solving this mystery!" she cried.

Suddenly, Mimi's cell phone rang to the tune of "Put Me on a Train Back to Texas." "We're heading back now," she said, snapping her cell phone shut. "*The General* is all ready to go."

In the taxi back to the Denver Temporary Station, Papa announced, "By this time tomorrow morning, we should arrive in Salt Lake City, Utah."

"Was Salt Lake City a stop on the Oregon Trail?" Grant asked.

"No, it wasn't," Mimi said, "but it was made popular by a guy named Hensley who found a safe trail that linked Salt Lake City to the California Trail."

Papa added, "Argonauts heading for California had a safe place to stop to replenish their supplies or live during the winter, when travel was too dangerous."

"That was back in the late 1840s?" Grant asked.

"Yes, when gold was discovered in California," Papa said.

"But space travel wasn't possible until the 1960s," Grant said.

"Oh, Grant!" Christina cried. "Seriously? Papa said *argonauts*, not *astronauts*!"

Grant frowned. "What is an argonaut, anyway?" he asked.

"They were the pioneers in search of gold!" Christina explained.

"Oh, OK, I got it," Grant said.

"So, Salt Lake City changed from a small, impoverished town to a prosperous one. Towns popped up all along that trail, and the state of Utah flourished as a whole," Mimi explained.

"Union Station!" the taxi driver announced.

Miss Tess met them at the station. "Hope you enjoyed your outing," she said. She looked flustered.

"Is everything OK, Miss Tess?" Mimi asked, grabbing the woman's arm.

The kids shadowed Mimi and Miss Tess, intending only to ask for ice cream. They overheard their conversation.

"What do you mean there were no tornado sightings in Kansas all week?" Mimi asked. "Are you sure?"

"Yes, ma'am," Miss Tess replied. "I was changing the newspaper liner in Petey's cage when I noticed the weather section. It turns out Kansas has been having excellent weather all week."

"Why would Luke make that up about the tornadoes?" Mimi asked. Her voice trailed off.

The kids raced to the private car. "Did you hear what Miss Tess said about Engineer Luke?" Anna asked Christina when they reached the private car.

"Yes! But why would he lie?" Christina returned.

"Well, he obviously wanted us to stay out of Kansas," Paul said.

"Maybe, Paul," Grant said. "Or he had another reason for changing the route."

21

DINAH, BLOW YOUR HORN!

Christina unrolled the gap-filled puzzle on Mr. Goodfellow's desk. Paul pulled out the remaining pieces from the journal and began filling in the blanks.

"Here's the last one," Christina said, handing Paul the piece with the message.

He read it. "Puzzled yet? The day's first light reveals all!"

"I guess we wait until sunup tomorrow," Christina said.

"Someone's coming!" Anna warned. Christina rolled up the puzzle and slid it into her backpack.

Mimi slid the door open. "In here again, I see!" she cried, then took a step back. "Ooh, teeth! Aside from Yogi Bear over here, it's pretty cozy in this car."

Grant mouthed the words 'Not Yogi Bear' and shook his head.

"Mimi, did you come to tell us lunch was ready?" Grant asked. "Because I'm starving!"

"Good, because Miss Tess is serving barbecue sandwiches and potato salad for lunch," she said. "See you in five minutes."

"Yes, ma'am!" the kids said as the door slid closed. Suddenly, they heard singing.

"I've been workin' on the railroad, All the live long day!"

"Papa?" Christina asked, looking around.

The singing continued, "I've been workin' on the railroad, Just to pass the time away. Don't you hear the whistle..."

"That's Papa!" Christina exclaimed. "I hear Papa!"

"Yes!" Grant said. "But from where?"

"Over here!" Paul cried. "Listen!"

"Dinah, blow your horn! Dinah, blow your horn! Dinah, blow your–" The music cut off suddenly.

"Here!" Paul said excitedly. He removed a framed picture from the wall.

"It's a speaker!" Anna said, amazed.

"Hmmm," Grant muttered, "Papa must have bumped into the button by accident."

"And then what, Inspector Grant?" Christina joked.

"Well, it's just a hunch, fellow inspectors, but if this car has a speaker, then wouldn't the other cars have one too?" he asked.

"Are you thinking what I'm thinking?" Christina asked her brother.

"If you're thinking that the bad guy is using it to scare us in the middle of the night, then, yes, I *am* thinking what you're thinking!" Grant exclaimed.

"Then there is no Danfy after all!" Anna said.

Paul fished a snack out of his pocket and gave it to Petey. "Oh, that reminds me, it's lunchtime!" Paul exclaimed.

22
A LEGACY TO PASS ON

After lunch, the children sat lazily around a table in the observation car. The girls read books, while the boys tried making houses out of cards.

"Paul, did you bring the journal?" Christina asked.

"I don't go anywhere without it," he said.

"We were so quick to find the puzzle clues that I wonder if we might have missed something," she said.

Anna asked, "Do you think anything good will come out of all of this?"

"Anna, I hope so," Christina answered. "Your great-great-grandfather went to a lot of trouble to make sure his legacy was passed on to your grandfather."

"Yes, but I doubt Grandpa even knows about the will, much less the treasure," Anna said.

"That's probably why your great-great-grandfather made finding the treasure so hard. He had to shroud its location in mystery just in case the will got into the wrong hands," Christina explained.

"I agree," Paul said, handing Christina the journal.

Christina opened it. "It's not a typical journal," she noted. She pulled at the spine of the journal. It slid off to reveal shallow compartments in both its front and back covers. Inside were an envelope and a photo.

"The envelope is still sealed," Christina remarked, "and it's labeled 'Authenticated Will of JMG.' It was sent to him by a law office."

"So the will that's floating around is only a copy," Paul guessed.

Christina nodded. "And there's a photo, too," she said.

"May I?" Anna asked.

Christina handed her the yellowing black-and-white photo. It showed five middle-aged men sitting around a card table smoking cigars.

"They look like they are all very good friends," Anna observed.

On the back of the photo, it read:

Winning Friendships
from l to r: John M. Goodfellow, John A. Goodfellow, Antonio (Tony) Calderas, Phineus Dunlop, Lawrence Grundwald

"This is Great-Great-Grandpa, and his son, our great-grandfather," Anna said, flipping the photo over to match the names to the faces.

"What about that Tony guy?" Grant wondered aloud. "Do you think your grandfather's assistant is related to this Tony?"

"I've never met Grandpa's assistant, but Grandpa often talks about how loyal Tony's family has been over the years," Paul said.

A photo? How could an old photo possibly have anything to do with solving this mystery? Christina wondered.

23

ALL PART OF THE PLAN!

"Wake up, Grant!" Christina said. "It's almost sunup!"

"I'm awake–just give me five more minutes," Grant begged and rolled over.

"Drastic times call for drastic measures! Ready, Paul?" Christina said.

"Ready!" Paul answered.

Christina grabbed Grant's feet. Paul grabbed his arms.

"Wait, stop! OK, I'm up! Gee whizz! Can't a guy get any sleep around here?" Grant squealed.

"Not when treasure is to be found!" Christina cried.

"Oh, yeah!" Grant said, remembering the puzzle clues.

The kids hurried to the private car.

Christina unrolled the completed puzzle. It shined a glittery gold.

"Look outside!" Anna cried. "It's beautiful!" The kids watched in awe as the horizon exploded into brilliant hues of pinks and purples.

"Now what do we do?" Anna asked.

"The morning light reveals all." Christina remembered the message. "Anna, Paul, let's hold it up to the window."

The sun rose slowly over the horizon. As the rays of the sun filtered through the paper, a large, rough drawing was revealed.

"It's a map–a map of *The General*!" Grant cried. "Look for yourselves!" Christina and Grant switched places with their friends.

"There is treasure hidden all over this train! See the gold symbol marks!" Paul exclaimed.

Suddenly, a man burst into the private car from the caboose. He kept his head down and his cap low over his eyes. By the time the kids registered what had just happened, the man had grabbed the map and was making his getaway!

"It's the thief! Grab him!" cried Grant.

Christina pushed the stuffed bear into the man, pinning him under it! The map was still clenched tightly in his grip. He pushed the heavy animal off him and reached for the door handle again to make his escape.

Just then, the door slid open and in walked Mimi and Papa, followed by Mr. Goodfellow.

The man took a step back when he saw the trio.

"Engineer Luke? What are you doing here?" Papa asked, confused.

The old man stood up to his full height. He was wearing a blue train engineer's uniform with a new black cap. There was an angry red gash across his forehead.

"I'll take that," Paul said, as he snatched the map out of the man's hand. The man reached to take it back, but Mr. Goodfellow stepped between them.

"Grandpa, the train is a moving treasure!" Paul said, handing the journal and the map to his grandfather.

"Tony," Mr. Goodfellow spoke calmly. "Why?"

"That's Tony, your assistant? Not Luke, the train engineer?" Mimi asked, shocked.

Tony appeared to shrink. He stared at the floor of the car.

"Grandpa, how did you know to come?" Paul asked.

"A very loyal friend named Gary tipped me off," Mr. Goodfellow said.

"Porter Gary! He was on the train platform before we left!" Christina exclaimed.

"He let me ride the baggage cart!" Grant said, smiling.

"Gary was trying to stop Tony from making a terrible mistake," Mr. Goodfellow explained. "Finding you all was a bit of a challenge, I must say."

"The fake weather report! The detour through Nebraska!" Christina exclaimed. "It was all part of the plan, wasn't it?"

Tony just stared at his own shoes.

"Did you leave those clues?" Grant asked.

Again, Tony just stared.

"Because you couldn't figure out what they meant for yourself?" Paul asked.

Tony kept his gaze to the floor. This time he nodded.

"You hired a replacement so you could monitor our progress. You never left the train, did you?" Anna asked.

Tony finally spoke. "The caboose was the safest place for me to hide from you. I only got off to..." he began. He looked at Grant.

"To run into me at the station!" Grant said accusingly.

Tony lifted his hand to his head.

"And when you wanted us gone, you made us believe there was a ghost on board!" Anna cried. "That was pretty mean!"

"But, why?" Mr. Goodfellow asked again. "We've known each other for as long as I can remember. How could you betray our long friendship?"

Tony lifted his icy-blue eyes and looked directly at Mr. Goodfellow. The **acrimony** in Tony's face took Mr. Goodfellow by surprise. He took a step back.

"John, it's true we've known each other since we were just kids," Tony said. "And my father knew your father, and so on. But can you honestly call what we have friendship? My family worked for your family. We were paid a **stipend** for our loyalty, but it never felt like real friendship!"

As Tony continued, his voice got louder. "It's as simple as that! I watched my father work two jobs to support our family, while yours grew wealthier and wealthier in the steel industry, first, and then in transportation! So, I wanted some of that back! My family deserves it!" Tony shouted.

Mr. Goodfellow was taken aback by what Tony just said. He stepped closer to Tony and said, "Good friend, I had no idea. I'm so sorry you feel that way."

24
IN THE RIGHT PLACE

Mimi, Papa, and Christina stretched out on the bleachers under the warm summer sun in Promontory Summit, Utah. Facing each other on a track were replicas of the Central Pacific's *Jupiter* and the Union Pacific's *No. 119*.

"This is where one era ended and where another one began!" Mimi said.

"And what an era it was!" Papa exclaimed. "You know, in Europe, where the steam locomotive had its beginnings, railroads linked already-existing towns and cities. That was very different from the role railroads played in the United States," he said.

"The railroads came first, and then the towns sprang up along those railroads, right?" Christina asked.

"Exactly!" Papa agreed. "And it was the steam train that made it possible for America to grow in the first place!"

"We shouldn't forget all the workers that laid all of this," Mimi said, pointing at the track in front of them. "They overcame enormous obstacles building the First Transcontinental Railroad, like blasting through the Sierra Nevada Mountains!"

"Or working through freezing weather and Indian attacks," added Papa. "Many men died building this railroad across the country."

"So what ever happened to the originals?" Christina asked, pointing to the locomotives in front of them.

"They were scrapped–if you can believe it!–the *No. 119* in 1903 and the *Jupiter* three years later," Papa said.

"That's sad," Christina said.

"You know, both the *Jupiter* and the *No. 119* were not originally picked to meet here for the Golden Spike ceremony on May 10, 1869," Mimi explained.

"Both happened to be in the right place at the right time," Papa said, winking at Christina.

"I know, Papa," Christina said. "If Grant and I hadn't been there on *The General*, things might have gone differently for Mr. Goodfellow."

On an adjacent track, Grant sped by in a handcar, his arms pumping fast. "Weee!" he screamed. He was grinning from ear to ear and waving.

Mimi waved back. "And to think Miss Tess and I were racking our brains trying to come up with fun things for you all to do!" she said. "Little did we know you kids were up to your ears in adventure!"

CLOMP! CLOMP! CLOMP! Grant climbed the bleachers to join them.

"Hey, did you see me?" Grant asked.

"Uh, you were kind of hard to miss, Grant!" Christina said.

"That was so fun!" Grant exclaimed.

"It did look like fun!" Mimi agreed.

"No, I mean the trip!" he corrected. "I loved every second of it!"

"Me, too!" Christina said.

"Well, now that Mr. Goodfellow doesn't have to sell his *treasured* train...get it?" Grant joked.

"Well, it was nice of Mr. Goodfellow to share some of his inheritance with his friend Tony, wasn't it?" Christina asked.

"It's too bad they had to go through all that to realize they were friends in the first place," Papa said.

Grant burst out laughing.

"What's so funny, Grant?" Christina asked.

"Just the look on Tony's face when Petey unlocked his own cage and flew around the room with that key in his mouth," Grant said. "SQUAAAAKK! SQUAAAKK!"

Christina giggled. "And how mad Tony was that he had been outsmarted by a bird!"

"Yep, that Petey outsmarted Tony when he hid the key under the newspaper liner!" Grant said.

Everyone laughed.

"Race you to the handcar?" Grant asked his sister.

"You're on!" Christina said, accepting the challenge.

Just then, she remembered racing Grant back through the train cars after the station dome closed.

It made her laugh out loud to think that back then, she had no idea she and her little brother were about to embark on a mystery that would unfold piece-by-piece as they rumbled across America!

Where shall we go next?

The End

Now...go to

www.carolemarshmysteries.com

and...

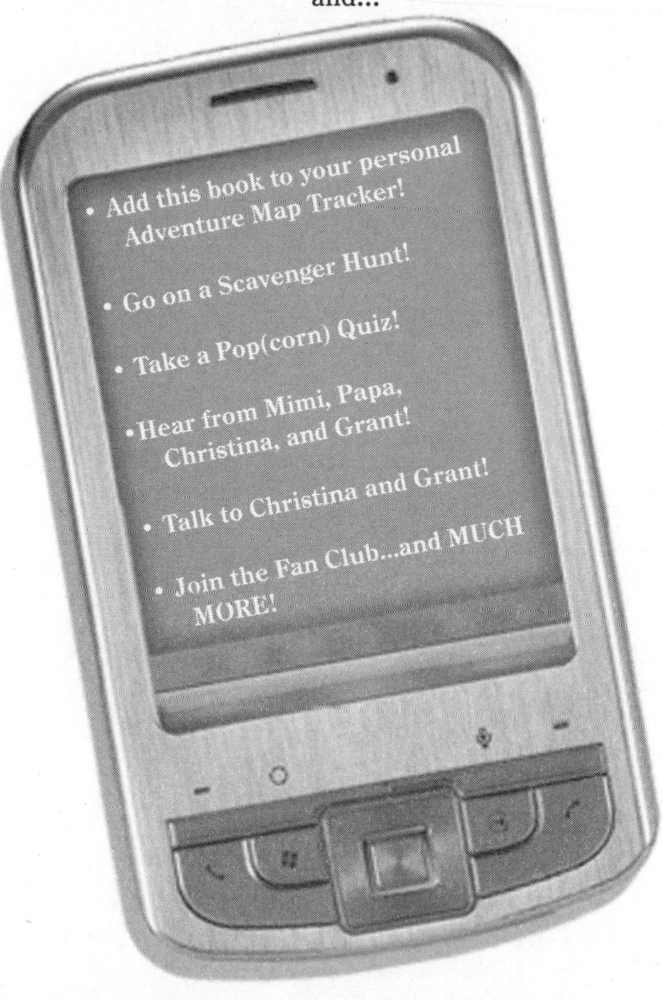

GLOSSARY

authenticated: confirmed to be genuine or valid

coincidence: a chance happening

destiny: events that are supposed to happen

feigned: pretended

inheritance: property or money passed down

itinerary: travel plan

landlocked: completely surrounded by land

obstacle: something that prevents progress

practical: useful

state-of-the art: the most advanced technology

SAT GLOSSARY

acrimony: bitterness, hostility

reprehensible: worthy of stern, strong disapproval

stipend: salary

vignette: decorative design

zenith: the highest point; peak

Enjoy this exciting excerpt from:

THE MYSTERY IN THE Twin Cities

1
MIMISODA

Grant had never worked so hard to get to a bathroom. He pulled his knee all the way to his chest and stretched his short leg.

CRRRUNCH! His royal blue boot disappeared into the snow's deep white cold.

"I'm never gonna make it," he whined, wishing he had listened to his big sister, Christina. She had warned him not to drink that soda.

Still, Grant had to snicker when he remembered the conversation that started his emergency. About an hour earlier, he had said to his grandmother, "Pass me a soda, please, Mimi." Mimi always made sure her red cooler was overflowing with drinks and snacks when they made a trip. It sat securely by her feet, mostly so Grant wouldn't make himself sick on the goodies.

With the steering wheel in the steady hands of Papa, the children's grandfather, Mimi had dozed off.

"Mimi, soda!" Grant had yelled to wake her. It had only taken him a second to get his own joke and he laughed hysterically. Even Papa couldn't stifle a belly laugh that roused Mimi from her slumber.

Christina had not been as quick. "What's so funny?" she had asked.

"That's where we're going!" Grant told her. "Mimisoda!"

Christina had rolled her eyes and told him, "Funny, Grant. I showed you the state at the top of the U.S. map. It's between North Dakota and Wisconsin, remember? You know it's Minnesota, not Mimisoda! And if you drink that soda, you'll be begging for a bathroom stop."

Grant's smile faded quickly when a howling wind tossed a blast of snow into his face. He wiped his eyes with his thick, blue mittens. The rest area restroom sign was still a good 10 or 15 giant steps away at the top of a small hill. The deep snowdrift circled it like a moat around a castle. *My kingdom for a drawbridge*, he thought, wishing for something solid and flat to walk on.

To keep his mind off his urgent need for the restroom, Grant concentrated on other things as he slogged through the snow. He listed all the fun activities he'd read about in a Minnesota travel brochure. He focused on his nose, which was so cold that the end of it was beating like a heart. He remembered the annoyed look Christina had shot him when he left on his bathroom journey and told her, "Promise I'll only be a minute."

Grant understood his sister's impatience. Several months earlier, Mimi and Papa invited them to come along on this January trip to Minnesota. At their Georgia home, they marked the days off their calendar with white paper snowflakes as a reminder of the wintry adventure ahead.

Mimi, a children's mystery book writer, had an idea for a Minnesota mystery. "I need to feel the bite of winter while the story's cooking in my head," she told them. Grant knew his grandmother cooked mysteries the way other grandmothers cooked casseroles. She'd add a bit of this and a dash of that until the delicious story was done.

Mimi gave the kids an even bigger surprise when she told them they could attend a famous festival–the Saint Paul Winter Carnival, also known as "The Coolest Celebration on Earth." Grant couldn't wait for it to start!

With one last giant effort, SMLOOOCH, Grant yanked his boot out of the snow and planted it on the concrete walkway. Salt, strewn to melt the snow, glittered like broken glass. He scampered to the green metal bathroom door as fast as his frozen feet could carry him. CREEEEEAK! The heavy door groaned open. Grant slipped inside and it slammed angrily behind him. Thrilled that no one was waiting in line, he dashed into a stall.

"WHEW!" Grant sighed as he made his way to the sink. "That's what I call relief!" His voice bounced eerily off the block walls before his face turned red. *Why did I say that out loud?* he wondered, and peeked quickly under the stalls for feet. There were none. He was all alone.

The bathroom was as cold as Mimi's freezer. Grant's breath came out in puffs of smoky vapor that floated away like chilly ghosts. The late afternoon sun, shining through the bony branches of a leafless tree, cast spooky shadows on the wall.

Grant wanted to run, but he could almost hear Mimi's voice ringing in his ears– "Don't forget to wash your hands!" The warm water felt like heaven to his cold, stinging fingers. He hummed *Walkin' Through a Winter Wonderland* to calm his nerves and let his eyes follow a curious gray crack along the red concrete floor. He imagined it was a river on the red planet, Mars. Mimi often told him his imagination would either make him a fine writer some day or get him into loads of trouble! So far, it had mostly been the latter.

Just as his imaginary Martian river reached the bathroom door, KA-POW! The door blasted open in a blinding ball of flashing fire.

Before Grant could move, an icy snowball clobbered him in the neck, and then exploded on the red concrete like a bag of spilled diamonds. Panicked, Grant thought, *I haven't even met anyone in Minnesota and already someone's out to get me!*

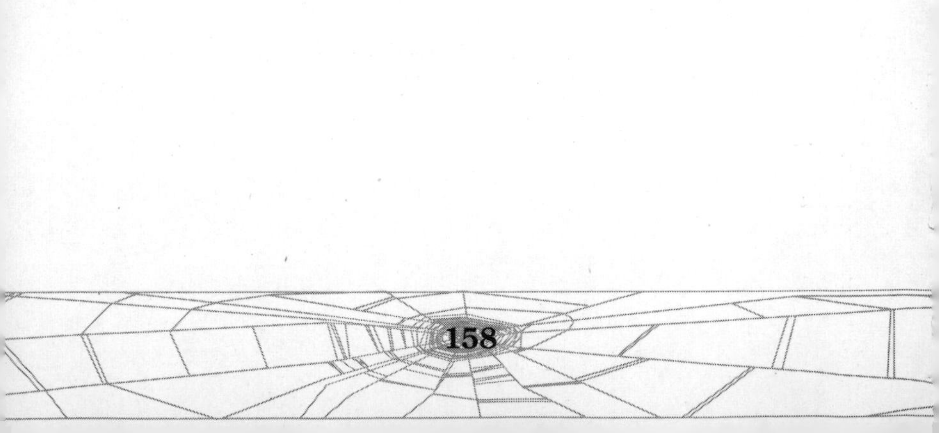